Jog, Frog, Jog

Written by
Barbara Gregorich

Illustrated by
Rex Schneider

This is a frog.

The frog likes to jog.

He jogs in the day.

He jogs in the night.

Oh, oh! This is a dog.

The dog does not like frogs.

The dog sees the frog!

Jog, frog, jog!

Jog in the water!

Jog in the fog!

Go, frog, go!

Jog into the log!

The log stops the dog.

Jog, frog! Jog around that dog!

Poor dog!